W9-BID-800

Andy Fox at School

by Fay Robinson
illustrated by Barry Rockwell

Roxy   Father   Mother   Andy

"Mother, I don't **want** to go to school," said Andy. "I want to stay with you."

"Come on, Andy.
You like school," said Mother.

"No, I don't!" he said.

"Good-bye, Andy,"
said Mother.
"Have a good day."

"Don't go, Mother!"
yelled Andy.

5

Mother gave Andy a hug.
"You will be fine," she said.
"Have fun with Mr. Bear.
I have to go now."

Andy sat on the rug
with his friends.
They sang and they clapped.

Andy made a web
with his friend Kit Cat.
Then they made a spider
for the web.

Andy read books.
He liked the big books
with cars and trucks best.

Andy ran up and down
with Kit Cat.
Kit ran as fast as she could.
But she did not catch Andy.
He ran very, very fast!

11

Andy played a math game
with Kit.
Andy won the game.
Kit won, too!

"Andy, your mother is here," said Mr. Bear.

"Mother, I don't **want** to go home," said Andy. "I want to stay at school."

"So you like school now?"
said Mother.

"I do like school," said Andy.
"But I like being with you,
   too."

"And I like being with **you**," said Mother.